21

Text copyright © 2021 Ana Siqueira

Illustrations copyright © 2021 Beaming Books

Published in 2021 by Beaming Books, an imprint of 1517 Media. All rights reserved.

No part of this book may be reproduced without permission from the publisher.

Email copyright@1517.media. Printed in the United States of America.

27 26 25 24 23 22 21   1 2 3 4 5 6 7 8

Hardcover ISBN: 978-1-5064-6810-5

Ebook IBSN: 978-1-5064-6895-2

Library of Congress Cataloging-in-Publication Data

Names: Siqueira, Ana, author. | Rodríguez, Geraldine, illustrator.
Title: Bella's recipe for success / by Ana Siqueira ; illustrated by
    Geraldine Rodriguez.
Description: Minneapolis, MN : Beaming Books, [2021] | Title on t.p. is
    Bella's recipe for disaster success with a line drawn through disaster.
    | Audience: Ages 3-8. | Summary: Bella has talented siblings but she is
    not sure what she is good at herself, so she goes on quest to discover
    her special gift and along the way learns the importance of never giving up.

Identifiers: LCCN 2020031888 (print) | LCCN 2020031889 (ebook) | ISBN
    9781506468105 (hardcover) | ISBN 9781506468952 (ebook)
Subjects: CYAC: Hispanic Americans--Fiction. | Grandmothers--Fiction. |
    Determination (Personality trait)--Fiction. | Baking--Fiction.
Classification: LCC PZ7.1.S5695 Be 2021 (print) | LCC PZ7.1.S5695 (ebook)
    | DDC [E]--dc23
LC record available at https://lccn.loc.gov/2020031888
LC ebook record available at https://lccn.loc.gov/2020031889

VN0004589: 9781506468105; JUN2021

Beaming Books
510 Marquette Avenue
Minneapolis, MN 55402
Beamingbooks.com

Bella's Recipe for ~~Disaster~~ SUCCESS

by Ana Siqueira

illustrated by Geraldine Rodríguez

beaming ☀ books

MINNEAPOLIS

I'm helping Abuela
in the kitchen, when . . .

"I can play the piano with my eyes closed!"
mi hermano brags.

"So what," mi hermana says. "I can do
fourteen cartwheels in a row."

Abuela says, "Oh, stop!
We're all good at different things."

We are? But what am I good at?

Maybe I can be a fabulosa gymnast like my sister.
But my somersaults are like jirafas rolling downhill.
Nope, not fabulosa.

Or maybe a great piano player like my brother?
But my hands are as heavy as elephants' feet.

And my music is not popular with my audience.
Nope, not great at all.

I know! I can be a baker like Abuela!

I beat and blend and mix and stir,
and the cookie dough is delici . . .

YUCKY! Salty.

I just discovered
something terrible!

I'm not good at anything!

I QUIT!

I cover my face
so nobody sees
my wet eyes.

But Abuela
sees everything.

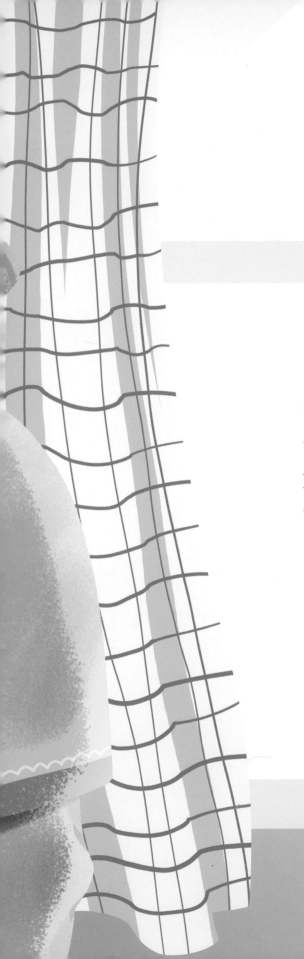

"Abuela," I say, "can you teach me how to make polvorones with dulce de leche?"

We beat, we blend, we bake.

But then I shout, "Oh, no! It's as hard as a rock!"

Abuela says, "Sometimes that happens, Bella. We can always try again."

Try again?

I bet my sister doesn't need to.

Then . . . CRASH!

"No biggie," mi hermana says.
"Everyone makes mistakes sometimes."

Not my brother.
He knows what he's doing.

Then . . . PLONK!

"Oops!" says mi hermano. "No hay problema.
I need more practice."

I can't believe it! Even mi hermano makes mistakes!

Hmm . . .

Maybe I can try again too!

I measure. I knead. I roll.

But my dough crumbles like sand.

OOPS, I forgot the egg.

No problem. Let's start over.

I add sugar, margarina, y vainilla.

Then, egg and flour. ¡MUY BIEN!

Time to finish the filling.

Stir, stir, stir without stopping.

Hmm . . .

I add more sugar and . . . OH NO!

My dulce de leche looks like cocodrilo skin.

Then I smell the cookies.

YUMMY!
¡DELICIOSOS!

My belly roars and I decide
to try one more time.

I'm extra careful this time.

I never stop stirring.

Wow! My dulce de leche is as smooth as a salamander.

And TA-DA!

My polvorones are deliciosos!

Finally, I'm good at baking and the master of . . .

PRACTICING.

No worries. Sometimes that happens.
We can always try again.

MAKE YOUR OWN POLVORONES CON DULCE DE LECHE

RECIPE FOR DULCE DE LECHE

Start with the dulce de leche so you can let it cool and thicken for one hour.

If you don't want to make it from scratch, you can buy premade dulce de leche.

INGREDIENTS:
4 cups whole milk
1½ cups sugar
1 teaspoon butter

ALTERNATIVES: If you like chocolate, add 2 tablespoons cocoa powder. If you like vanilla, add 2 teaspoons vanilla.

INSTRUCTIONS:
- Stir together milk, sugar, and butter in a saucepan.
- Bring to a boil.
- Reduce heat.
- Stir frequently, especially after it starts to thicken.
- It is ready when it thickens (about 1½ hours).
- Transfer to a bowl to cool for about one hour.

RECIPE FOR POLVORONES
Servings: 16 cookies.

INGREDIENTS:
1½ cups all-purpose flour
½ cup shortening
½ cup sugar
1 teaspoon baking powder
2 teaspoons vanilla
1 egg

INSTRUCTIONS:
- Beat the flour, shortening, sugar, and baking powder.
- Add the vanilla and egg.
- Mix all until your dough is not too dry and it doesn't stick to your hands.
- Wrap the dough in plastic wrap and place in the refrigerator for one hour.

  - If it's too dry, add some shortening.
  - If it's too wet, add some flour.

- Roll the dough into little balls, then flatten them a little so they look like discs.
- While flattening, keep your thumb in the top middle so it makes a little indent for the dulce de leche.
- Bake for about 10–15 minutes at 400 degrees F.
- When the cookies are done, use a pastry bag to fill the indent with dulce de leche.

NOTE: Another option is to skip the hole in the cookies and make cookie sandwiches instead, with polvorones on the outside and dulce de leche in the center.

ABOUT THE AUTHOR AND ILLUSTRATOR

ANA SIQUEIRA is a Spanish-language elementary teacher and an award-winning children's book author based in Tampa, Florida. Before *Bella's Recipe for Success*, she published children's books in Portuguese in Brazil and and in Spanish in foreign language educational markets. Ana is also a global educator, a PBS Media innovator, and an SCBWI member.

GERALDINE RODRÍGUEZ is a Mexican illustrator and digital artist who enjoys telling stories through colors and lines. In addition to *Bella's Recipe for Success*, Geraldine is the illustrator of *Cinco de Mayo* and the Adventures of Samuel Oliver series.